goes to the Aquarium

Written by

Miles Mayweather

To My Bright and Shining Stars,
May your imaginations remain unbounded and forever render the weight of the world as light as a feather.

Love, Dad

Published in association with
Bear With Us Productions

© 2023

The right of Miles Mayweather as the author of this work has been asserted by him in accordance with the Copyright Designs and Patents Act 1988.
All rights reserved, including the right of reproduction in whole or part in any form.

ISBN: 979-8-218-14676-4

Cover by Yogesh Mahajan
Illustrated by Yogesh Mahajan

www.justbearwithus.com

Cory the Car
goes to the Aquarium

Written by

Miles Mayweather

Illustrated by

Yogesh Mahajan

Cory was a little girl.

Not just any NORMAL little girl.

During the day Cory **loved** to play with her toy vehicles.

She had lots of them –

BIG ONES,

small ones.

She had an

ENORMOUS collection

and each and every one had a story to tell.

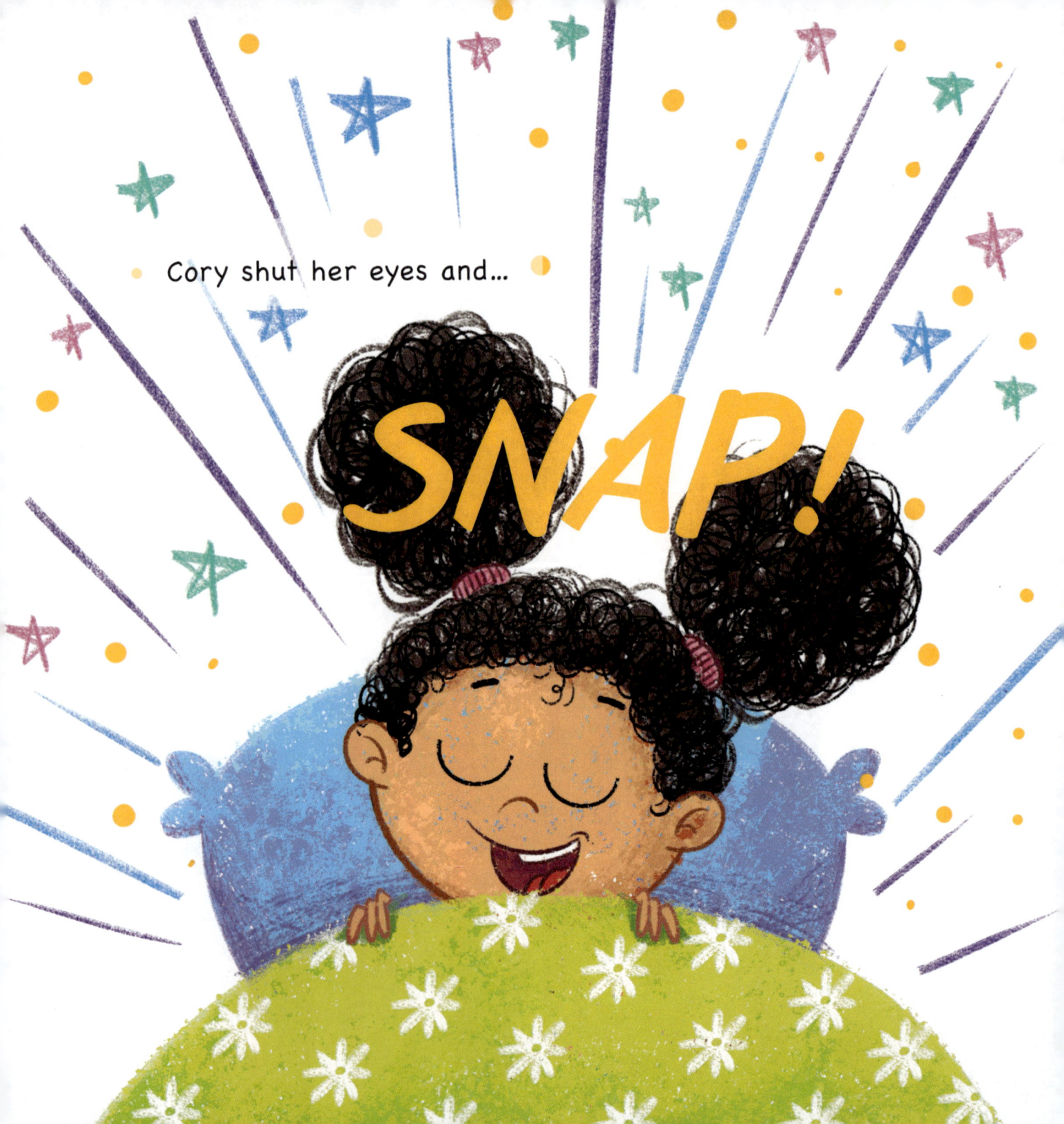

Just like that, she wasn't a little girl anymore.

Surrounded by her little adventuring vehicles,
Cory herself became a car.

Not just any car, but the SHINIEST, most fantastic car

that has EVER existed.

Cory went on many **wonderful adventures** with all of the vehicles she saw around the neighborhood, just like the ones she played with during the day.

On this particular night, Cory was *zooming* up and down the block, spinning her wheels and whooping.

She loved being so *Fast* and zippy.

"Hey Cory!" called Tommy the Trash Truck as he trundled down the road.

"Hey Tommy!" replied Cory, "Look how shiny my wheels are!"

"Wow-ee!" Tommy marveled.

"What's that?" Cory asked as she pointed to a piece of seaweed dangling from the top of Tommy's trash chute. "Oh, I had to take out the trash from the aquarium." Tommy said.

"The aquarium!" cried Cory, "Cool! I love fish!"

"Let's go!" Tommy whooped, and he and Cory zoomed down to the aquarium.

"Look at their funny mouths," giggled Cory.

"And their flappy little fins!" Tommy agreed.

"Which one is your favorite, Tommy?" Cory asked.

She was watching a **wiggly**, **jiggly** octopus swim across a tank.

"I like the puffer fish," Tommy said proudly, "they eat anything and everything - just like me!"

"Well, I like the sailfish," Cory **zoomed** over to where the sailfish was swimming back and forth.

"They're the ***FASTEST*** fish in the oceans, just like I'm the ***FASTEST*** car on the road!"

Cory and Tommy **loved** looking at the fish. There were all sorts *gliding* back and forth in their tanks.

Cory yawned.

This adventure was great,

but it was making her tired.

"Time to go home?" Tommy suggested.

Together, they drove back to Cory's house.

"See you again tomorrow night," said Tommy.

"Good night!" Cory blipped her lights in farewell.

Cory woke up again as a little girl the very next morning.

"Mom, Dad!" she called, "You'll never guess what happened in my dream!"

Mom and Dad sat on Cory's bed and listened to all of her adventures at the aquarium. Cory couldn't *wait* to see what adventure she would go on *tomorrow* night!

...And neither could Tommy!

Made in the USA
Middletown, DE
02 August 2024